Living Sustainably

Heather Rising

Contents

Living Sustainably

Living for the Future

Earth is the only known planet with lush forests, sparkling rivers, deep oceans and air to breathe. However, human activities have increased harmful **greenhouse gases** by burning coal, oil and gas. These gases pollute the air and contribute to warmer temperatures. Higher temperatures on Earth are melting polar **ice caps** and causing extreme weather.

In 2015, nearly every country in the world supported what was called the "Paris Agreement". These countries agreed to a **net-zero** release of greenhouse gases by 2050, to prevent world temperatures from increasing even more. To achieve this goal, people all over the world will need to live more sustainably.

Students at a sustainable school help out by watering the vegetable garden.

Living sustainably means living in ways that do not harm the environment. Sustainable living can allow people to grow up, go to school or work, enjoy their free time and visit places in the world while leaving the planet unharmed for the future.

The decade between 2011 and 2020 was the warmest on record. Greenhouse gases are the main cause. These gases surround Earth and prevent the Sun's heat from escaping back into space.

Sustainable Schools

Building Sustainable Schools

Sustainable schools have been built all over the world, constructed with local materials. This means large amounts of greenhouse gases don't need to be released to transport the materials a long distance. The materials used to build sustainable schools are also **renewable**.

In Indonesia, the school building and furniture at The Green School have been constructed from locally grown bamboo. Bamboo grows in as little as three years, making it quick to replace and a good sustainable resource.

The Green School in Indonesia is built from renewable bamboo.

To reduce the need for electric lights, designers of sustainable schools take advantage of natural lighting using **skylights** and **insulated** windows. Another way to make a school more sustainable is to install a "green roof". This type of roof has a layer of living plants which acts as insulation, reducing the power needed to heat or cool the building. Covering the roof in native plants also provides habitat for insects and birds, and absorbs rainwater, reducing the risk of floods.

A green roof is a layer of living plants on the roof of a building.

One primary school in Kenya has a roof that collects rainwater and directs it to an underground storage tank. The water is used to supply the school vegetable gardens, which provide food for students and a habitat for other living things.

Students take care of their school vegetable garden.

Sustainable School Grounds

Many other schools are making changes to contribute positively to the environment and become more sustainable. Some schools have garden boxes to grow trees or vegetables on the school ground.

One primary school in Melbourne, Australia, hung planter boxes around their covered sports area. The plants clean the air and provide extra shade to keep students cool.

Planter boxes hung in this covered school sports area help to clean the air.

Methane is a greenhouse gas that is produced when **organic** waste decomposes, or breaks down. More methane is produced when there is less oxygen available while waste is decomposing, such as in a landfill.

At many schools, student clubs maintain composters to break down vegetable and fruit scraps from snacks and lunches. This keeps the waste out of landfills, reducing methane **emissions**, and the composted nutrients can also be added to school gardens.

Students tip food waste into their school's composter.

Energy Use at School

A large part of a school's **carbon footprint** comes from the energy used to heat or cool the buildings. Energy made by burning coal or oil adds carbon dioxide to the atmosphere. Solar panels or wind turbines can be installed in schools to reduce greenhouse gases.

One primary school in Western Australia raised $28 000 in donations from the community to buy new solar panels. They were able to install 80 new solar panels.

Turning off lights when the classroom is empty, or setting electronic screens to turn off when inactive, are other ways to reduce electricity usage. In addition, small, inexpensive solar panels can be used to recharge class devices, timers and clocks.

A secondary school in Hong Kong uses a combination of solar and wind turbines to generate power. They also put motion detectors on their lights so the lights only turn on when needed.

This school in Hong Kong is powered by solar panels and wind turbines.

Getting to School

Walking, riding bikes or using public transport to get to school reduces the number of kilometres students need to travel in cars, reducing the amount of petrol used. Each litre of petrol burned as fuel can create 2.3 kilograms of carbon dioxide emissions.

Many schools around the world operate a "walking bus". In a walking bus, volunteers choose a safe drop-off place near the school to meet students. The group walks the last stretch together, reducing the distance travelled in a vehicle.

Students in a walking bus often wear high-visibility vests for safety.

School Materials

Schools can become more sustainable by using materials that are less harmful to the environment. Plastic is made from oil, a fossil fuel. Using reusable metal bottles reduces plastic use. So does using erasers made from natural **latex** instead of plastic. Glitter is a type of plastic and it washes easily into oceans, so using edible glitter made from sugar for craft projects instead is more environmentally friendly. Schools that buy pencils made from bamboo, or mechanical pencils that only need **graphite**, help prevent deforestation.

Using glitter made from sugar for craft projects is more sustainable than using plastic glitter.

If digital textbooks are used in schools, fewer paper books are needed and fewer trees need to be cut down. Old textbooks can be donated to other schools or sent to be recycled. Buying paper for notebooks and art that is made from 100 per cent recycled materials is another way to help save forests.

It is estimated that over 8 million trees are chopped down every year to make pencils, and 9 billion plastic pens end up in landfills each year.

Using digital textbooks is one way schools can help to reduce the number of trees that need to be cut down for paper.

Recycling at School

The aim of a sustainable school is to produce zero waste. Students are asked to bring food to school in reusable containers and drink from reusable bottles. Any food scraps are composted at school.

Materials in sustainable schools are often reused before they are recycled. School projects are dismantled and the usable paper is sorted and stored to be used again. Once the paper or other material is no longer good for projects, it is sent to be recycled.

Recycling centres can be set up in schools to make it easier for students to sort materials. Batteries, metals, plastics, cloth and glass can all be recycled. Any school can set up reusing and recycling programs.

Sorting waste into different bins at school allows some waste to be recycled.

Landfills are full of plastic waste.
Many waterways are clogged with plastic waste.
Only 9 per cent of all the plastic that has been produced has been recycled. The rest is filling up landfills and waterways. It has been estimated that 8 million tonnes of plastic enter our oceans each year.

A Sustainable Curriculum

The **curriculum** at a sustainable school includes a focus on environmental issues, such as reducing the use of fossil fuels. School projects centre on improving conditions in the community, by doing such things as creating a neighbourhood garden or planting trees. Any school can adapt their curriculum to include some of these ideas.

At a school in North Carolina, USA, a fourth-grade class created a renewable energy classroom. During their Energy unit, students calculated how much energy they used, then worked to create that energy from 100 per cent renewable sources. The result was a solar- and wind-powered classroom, built using funds they raised themselves.

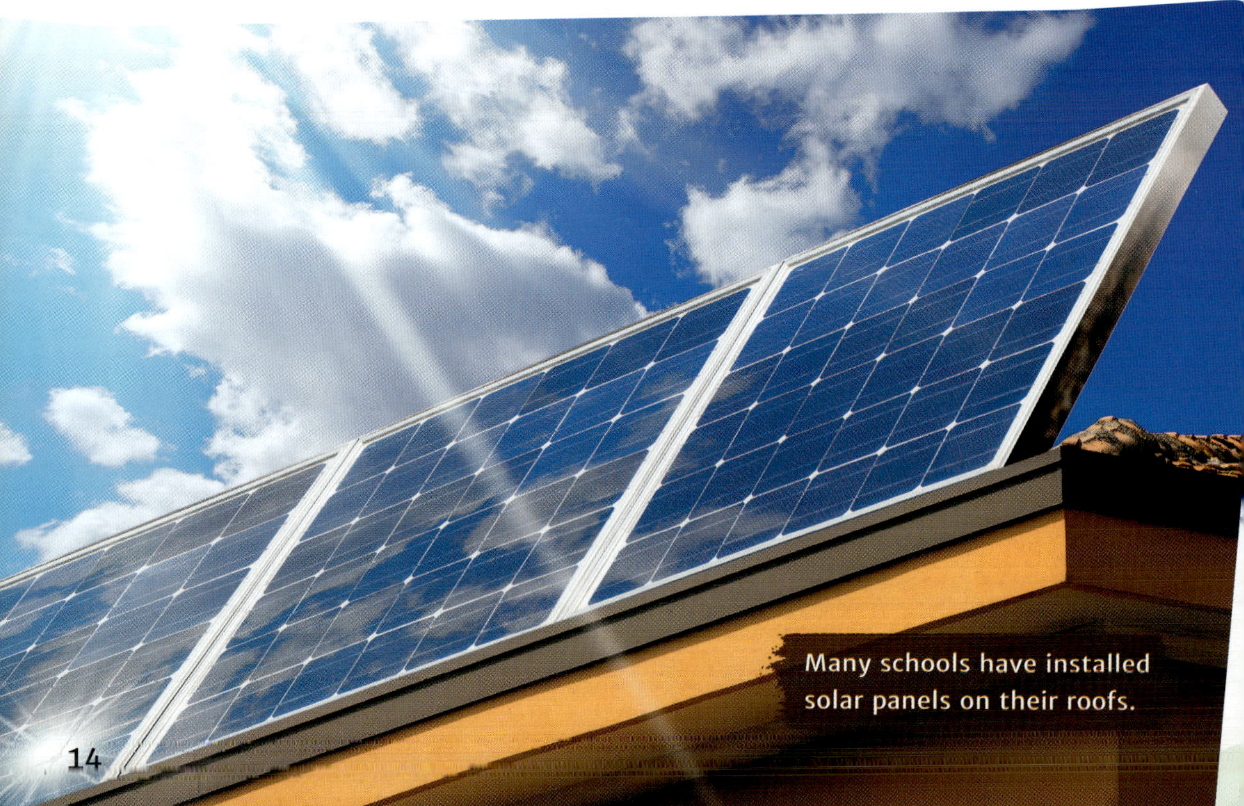

Many schools have installed solar panels on their roofs.

What can your class do this year to reduce its carbon footprint?

Students on the Environment Committee at a secondary school in Melbourne, Australia, raised awareness in their school community about the damage caused by single-use plastic water bottles. The group raised funds to buy a filtered drinking fountain so that students could refill their bottles. Their school has reduced packaged water bottles by 50 per cent.

A school in rural New Zealand had a problem with rodents, such as rats, nesting in their recycling area. After the students conducted research into how to fix the problem, they applied for a **grant** to purchase composters with lids, as well as the materials for a worm composter. In class, the students collected data on the benefits and drawbacks of the two types of composters. Since they began composting the organic waste at school, the rodents have disappeared.

Worm composters are a great way to recycle organic waste at school or at home.

Sustainable Homes

Building Sustainable Homes

Energy-efficient homes are being built all around the world. These homes are smaller, and the interiors are designed to be heated or cooled using less power. Planners consider the direction the windows face, in order to take advantage of the heat from the Sun in cold climates, or reduce exposure to its rays in warm ones.

Sustainable homes are also well-insulated to prevent too much heat from entering or escaping the building. In warm climates, the roofs may hold solar water heaters or solar panels. In areas where flooding is a risk, green roofs hold native plants which absorb rainwater, reducing the chance of floods.

Builders of sustainable homes choose recycled materials, such as wood, metal or brick, or use wood from sustainable forests, where each tree cut down is replaced with a new sapling. The furniture inside the homes is built from plant products, such as cane, and decorations are manufactured from wool or glass, which can be replenished or recycled.

These sustainable homes have living green roofs.

Features of a Sustainable Home

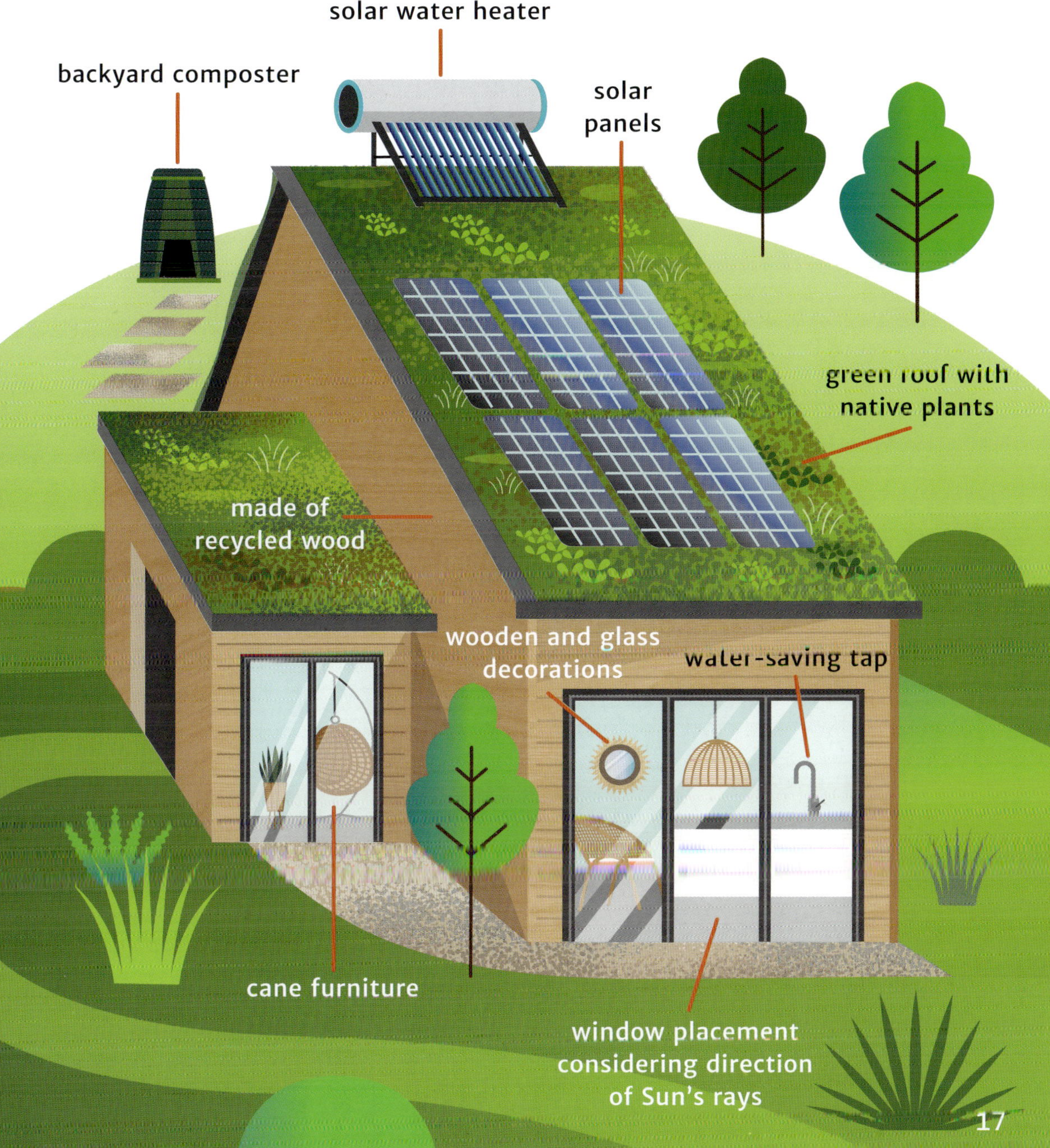

Conserving Resources

Sustainable homes are designed to **conserve** resources such as energy and water. Different types of heating and cooling systems that make homes more sustainable, such as heat pumps that use **geothermal** energy, are becoming more popular. Underfloor heating works at lower temperatures than other kinds of heating, meaning that energy use is reduced by more than 15 per cent.

In any home, it is possible to reduce how much energy is used for heating and cooling by simply lowering blinds on hot days to block the Sun's rays, and doing the opposite on cool days to let the rays warm the room.

People can save electricity if they switch off lights when they don't need them, and use low-energy light bulbs, like **LEDs**. Using small solar chargers to power phones and video game controllers is another way to reduce greenhouse gas emissions by saving energy.

Less energy-efficient light bulbs can be replaced with LEDs.

Conserving water helps to prevent habitat destruction to make way for new **reservoirs**, and it also reduces harmful emissions. Pumping and filtering waste water takes energy. An average shower head releases 12 litres of water per minute. If everyone shortened their shower by one or two minutes, it would save many litres of water. Turning off the tap when brushing their teeth is another way people can decrease the water they use.

Water-saving toilets and taps reduce water usage. Most dishwashers and washing machines have economy settings that use less water and electricity. Other changes people can make to their habits, such as only running the dishwasher when it's full and wearing clothes more than once before washing them if they are not dirty, also conserve water resources.

When new reservoirs are created, large areas of land are flooded, destroying wildlife habitats.

Small Changes

Whether people live in houses or in apartments, there is always a bit of space that can be used to make small changes to live more sustainably. Balconies can hold planter boxes with vegetables or with native plants that provide habitat for insects. Countertop worm composters can break down fruit and vegetable scraps, while providing fertiliser for house plants. Outdoor composters fit in small spaces and can decompose garden waste, such as flowers and grass clippings.

Vegetables can be grown in balcony planter boxes.

Separate containers can be set up in the home for recyclable materials, making it easy to make sure they are separated into the right collection bins for recycling. Many household items can be reused or donated, such as old clothes and toys.

So many items available today are made from recycled materials. Buying toothbrushes, toys and clothing made from recycled plastic, paper or cloth is a more sustainable way to live.

People can separate waste into different bins in their homes to help with recycling.

Recycling 1000 kilograms of paper can save about 37 000 litres of water and 17 trees, and prevent 27 kilograms of air pollutants being released.

Sustainable Cities

Moving Around a Sustainable City

One of the largest producers of air pollution in a city is vehicle traffic. Redesigning how people move around a city can reduce air pollution and make the city more sustainable. Adding bike paths, pedestrian zones and safe footpaths can encourage people to leave their cars at home.

A bus often carries as many people as 40 individual cars. Buses and trains that run on clean fuel, such as electricity made from sustainable sources, can reduce greenhouse gases. Making public transport in the city affordable means more people will use it, reducing the number of vehicles on the roads.

Features of a Sustainable City

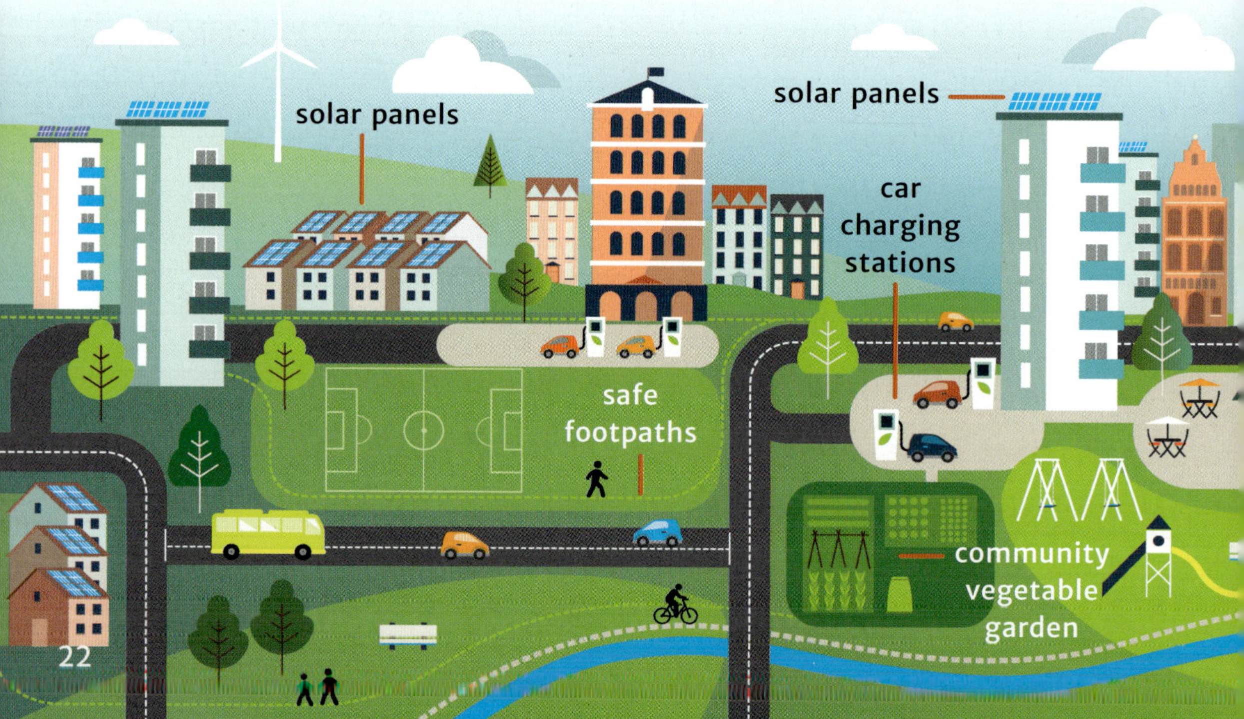

Providing spaces where bikes and electric scooters can be easily rented is another way to encourage people not to drive. Making new laws restricting pollution or taxing people who drive individual cars can also discourage people from driving in the city. Finally, installing electric charging stations around the city supports people using electric vehicles.

By 2050, Iceland plans to convert all its public buses to run on clean-burning hydrogen fuel.

In the city of Copenhagen, Denmark, bike paths and bridges for bikes and pedestrians were built over waterways throughout the city. Now, more than 60 per cent of the city's residents travel to work or school by bike. In 2015, the city of Dubai, United Arab Emirates, completed construction of a sustainable neighbourhood where 100 per cent of the waste and water is recycled. The area is car-free, and the centre of the space is filled with greenhouses for urban gardening.

Green Space

Adding trees and green spaces to a city is a way to remove carbon dioxide from the air after it has been emitted. During **photosynthesis**, trees release oxygen and filter carbon dioxide out of the air. Trees also make water vapour and provide shade, both of which help cool a city.

The city of Melbourne, Australia, is planning to create five new parks and conservation areas to increase the number of trees in the city. The city is also funding research into the science and technology of green roofs.

Trees and green spaces help to make Melbourne, Australia, a more sustainable city.

When planning new developments in a city, it is important to set aside space for community gardens. The city of Washington, D.C., in the USA, provides public space for gardens as well as financial grants to cover the costs of setting them up. There are now enough urban gardens in the city to supply the local restaurants with vegetables.

The town of Todmorden, England, has urban vegetable gardens at every school, at the police station, at cemeteries and the railway station, totalling around 40 different gardens.

In areas where heavy rainfall is normal, keeping enough green spaces to absorb rain can prevent flooding and erosion.

Residents work in a community vegetable garden in the US city of Washington, D.C.

Waste Management

While many cities already have recycling programs for plastic and paper, waste-management programs can further reduce landfill use by collecting a wider variety of materials, such as metal or wood, or organic waste.

The city of Toronto, Canada, has a population of almost 3 million, and its waste-management department collects all food and organic waste, including soiled paper and pet waste, from residents. The materials are put in large containers called "digesters", where the material is specially treated to make it break down into its smallest parts. The process produces fertiliser, which is used in the city parks, and bio-gas, which is used to heat buildings.

In 1950, Germany had 50 000 landfill sites. Through efficient methods of sorting materials and recycling, including composting of organic waste, by 2017 there were only 300 left.

The city of Toronto, Canada, uses huge digesters to break down organic waste.

Human activity has changed Earth's climate. If countries are to reach net-zero emissions by 2050, as they promised to do in the Paris Agreement, people all around the world will need to live more sustainable lives.

Schools can help by doing things such as building with local, renewable materials and setting up recycling and composting programs in the school ground. In their own homes, people can help by doing things such as building smaller and more energy-efficient homes, installing solar panels or putting planter boxes on their balconies. And cities can help everyone to live more sustainable lives by making it easy for people to drive less, use less energy, recycle and breathe clean air.

What changes can you make to reduce your carbon footprint and live more sustainably?

How to Set Up a Worm Composter

Many schools are setting up systems to compost food scraps and reduce the waste sent to landfills. In some places, ordinary composters can attract unwanted rodents, or release unpleasant odours. A worm composter eliminates those problems and provides nutrients more quickly for gardens. Follow these instructions to construct your own worm composter at home or at school.

Goal

To set up a worm composter

Materials

- 2 large stackable plastic tubs with 1 lid
- drill
- gardening gloves
- worm bedding, e.g. dry leaves, potting soil and shredded cardboard
- a bag of compost worms
- worm food, e.g. fruit and vegetable scraps, egg shells, tea leaves or coffee grounds (no citrus fruit, meat or dairy)
- a watering can.

Steps

1. Ask an adult to use the drill to make tiny holes in the bottom of the first tub, and bigger air holes in the lid.
2. Place worm bedding into the first tub until it is three-quarters full. Make sure you have some bedding left over.
3. Stack the first tub inside the second tub. The second tub will collect liquid.
4. Sprinkle some water on the worm bedding. Put on the gardening gloves and use your hands to mix the bedding until it is moist and loose.
5. Tip the worms on top of the mixed bedding.

6. Place the worm food on top, spreading it out into a layer over the worms.
7. Cover the worm food with more worm bedding. Put the lid on.
8. Lift the lid each day to check on your composter, adding water when needed to keep it moist. Add a bit more worm food each day, too, and cover it with bedding.
9. Once the worms have digested the food, a liquid will drain out of the holes into the bottom tub. Mix this nutrient-rich liquid with plenty of water and use it to feed the plants in your garden.
10. Once a month, use your hands (wearing gloves) to carefully turn the soil in your worm composter. Add new worm bedding if necessary.

Glossary

carbon footprint (*noun*)	the amount of greenhouse gases produced by the actions of one person or group
conserve (*verb*)	to use as little of something as possible, e.g. energy
curriculum (*noun*)	the subjects that are taught in a school
emissions (*noun*)	gas released into the air
energy-efficient (*adjective*)	not requiring very much energy to work
geothermal (*adjective*)	using heat from under the ground
grant (*noun*)	money given by an organisation such as a government to be used for a specific purpose
graphite (*noun*)	a soft black mineral used in the middle of pencils
greenhouse gases (*noun*)	the gases that contribute to climate change, especially carbon dioxide and methane
ice caps (*noun*)	layers of permanent ice
insulated (*adjective*)	protected with a material that stops heat escaping or entering
latex (*noun*)	a white substance produced by some plants and trees that can be used to make erasers and other products
LEDs (*noun*)	Light Emitting Diodes: special light bulbs that are very energy efficient

net-zero (*adjective*) balanced so that the same number of emissions are entering and being removed from the atmosphere

organic (*adjective*) to do with living things

photosynthesis (*noun*) the process by which plants take in carbon dioxide from the air

renewable (*adjective*) able to be naturally replaced; not all used up

reservoirs (*noun*) large lakes used for human water supply

skylights (*noun*) small windows in a roof

Index